Curious George
Librarian for a Day

Adaptation by Julie Tibbott
Based on the TV series teleplay written by Scott Gray

Houghton Mifflin Harcourt
Boston New York 2012

For information about permission to reproduce selections from this book, write to Permissions,
Houghton Mifflin Harcourt Publishing Company, 215 Park Avenue South, New York, New York 10003.

Library of Congress Cataloging-in-Publication Data is on file.

ISBN: 978-0-547-85282-9 paper-over-board
ISBN: 978-0-547-85281-2 paperback

Design by Afsoon Razavi
www.hmhbooks.com
Manufactured in China
LEO 10 9 8 7 6 5 4 3 2 1
4500354688

AGES	GRADES	GUIDED READING LEVEL	READING RECOVERY LEVEL	LEXILE ® LEVEL
5–7	2	J	17	480L

George goes to the library once a week.
This time the librarian, Mrs. Dewey,
asked George to help her.

Mrs. Dewey gave George a cart.
It held books and DVDs.
George had to sort them into two pile
George was super fast!

Then Mrs. Dewey
had to leave in a hurry. Her
book club needed her. She put
George in charge of the library!

George wondered. Should he put
the books away?
It seemed like something a
monkey in charge would do.

George put the books away in
record time.
This librarian stuff was easy.

Then the doorman came into the library. "Hi, George," said the doorman. "Can you help me find my dog Hundley's favorite book? It's a yellow book."

George was very
familiar with that color.
The yellow books George found
were not the right ones.
There were a lot of yellow books!

Finally, George found the right book.
"Thanks, George!" said the doorman.

Finding books was
hard! George was curious.
Would the books be easier to find if
they were sorted by color?

After George sorted the books, Chef
Pisghetti came in.
"I can't find my cat Gnocchi's favorite
book, *Mice Everywhere*," he said.

George just needed
to know what color the book was.
The chef didn't know the book's color.
He did know that it was very, very big!

13

George looked for a big book.
There were big books in every color!
At last, George found the right one.
It was heavy.
"Thanks, George," said the chef.

George decided to try putting the books in order of size: little books, medium books, big books.
George had fixed the library again!

But then Steve needed help too.
"George, the books are all messed up!"
Steve said. "This is where all the outer
space books are supposed to be."

George showed how he had sorted
the books by size.
"I don't think that's how libraries
work," Steve said.
He showed George where all of
the books about outer space were
supposed to be.
This made George even more
curious.

George wondered: If all the outer space books go together, maybe books are organized by subject. Steve said the subject is what the book is about.

George needed to fix the library
again before Mrs. Dewey came back.
Steve helped George sort the books
by subject.

"It's neat as a pin in here!" Mrs. Dewey said when she returned. She explained that books are arranged by subject, and then alphabetically by the author's last name.

Alphabetically means in the same order as the letters of the alphabet.
Names that start with the letter A come before names that start with B.
And names that start with Z go last.
Z is the last letter of the alphabet.

George had had fun helping at the
library.
But he was happy to go home with his
own favorite book!

Color and Size Scavenger Hunt!

You and a friend can learn about sorting just like George did!

- Pick a color with your friend.

- Together, find five items of that color. For example, if you picked the color green, you might find a blade of grass, a green apple, a green toy, a green sock, or a green cup. Make sure a grownup has given you permission to collect the items for your scavenger hunt!

- Let one person organize the items by size, biggest to smallest.

- Now let the other person put the items in alphabetical order, from A to Z. Do you have any items that begin with the letter A? Now you've learned to organize, just like George!

One of these is not like the others!

George learned that library books are organized by subject. That means books that are about the same thing go together. Look at the rows of pictures below. Each row shows three items that are similar and one that is different. Try to pick out the picture that does not belong. What do the other three items have in common?

Row 1: The man with the yellow hat; row 2: flowers; row 3: sailboat; row 4: baseball bat